The Day The World Stood Still

Instagram: @scepsisters

ISBN 978-1-7774033-0-0

The world is a busy place
and everyone is always running around.

There is always something to do,

someone to see,
or somewhere to be.

The people are in a rush.

Their fingers are scrolling,

cameras always rolling,

and screen time is soaring.

The people are distracted.

The parks are packed, the streets are crowded, and the stores are overflowing.

The people make so much noise.

The cars are zooming, the ships are sailing, and the planes are flying.

The people are lost.

They pollute the air, poison the water, and abuse the land.

The people are destroying the Earth.

One day, the germ came and everything began to change.

Turning homes into hideouts,

high fives and handshakes into waves from a distance,

and hugs and kisses into phone calls and window visits.

This is when the world stood still.

Many places closed and the people started learning in new ways.

Mrs. Smith's stuffy indoor science class is being taught outdoors by Mother Nature.

Long hours at work for parents are now late evenings surrounded by family at the dining room table.

The fast moving people
are slowing down.

The people have changed the way they use technology. Screens full of emptiness are now reconnecting loved ones near and far. Pointless social media posts are replaced with opportunities to support each other. Likes lead to donations, comments are full of encouragement, and shares allow smiles to be spread across the globe.

The people are connecting.

Finally have time to read again. Does anyone have good recommendations?

My Grandma is teaching me some new Turkish recipes!

Really missing everyone at home but today's hike was amazing.

Only important places are allowed to be open.
The crowded stores are empty, the people only
buy things they need.

The restaurants once full of chaos are now
home to take out boxes and porch deliveries.

The children who filled
parks and playgrounds
create their own fun
using their imaginations.

The people are quiet.

Travel around the world begins to look different. The cars that were stuck in traffic, lead birthday parades and deliver gifts to family and friends.

The ships which moved through the ocean are docked, letting people discover the magic of their own country.

Plane seats filled with people now deliver emergency supplies to those in need.

The people are finding purpose.

People staying home, allows the Earth to slowly heal.

The poisoned lakes and oceans sparkle, the streets are still,

and the animals return to places they once called home.

The land is being used to plant seeds for future picking. Bringing peace to those discovering the hidden treasures of the forest.

The thick, dark fog that filled the air now fades away to show the crisp blue sky.

The people understand their impact.

HOSPITAL
Thank you health workers
Good work
Police
Thank you
Donations
01

There are people who say the germ brought terrible things to the world and the germ should not have come and changed everything.

These people are right, everything changed.

We, the people began to move a little slower, act a little kinder, grow a little stronger, and love a little harder.

The world came together as the people stayed apart. The germ taught us how to be still in a time of chaos.

We realized the new world which we discovered was far greater than the world we left behind.